Silas Weir Mitchell

The hill of stones

And other poems

Silas Weir Mitchell

The hill of stones
And other poems

ISBN/EAN: 9783743328433

Manufactured in Europe, USA, Canada, Australia, Japa

Cover: Foto ©Andreas Hilbeck / pixelio.de

Manufactured and distributed by brebook publishing software
(www.brebook.com)

Silas Weir Mitchell

The hill of stones

THE HILL OF STONES

AND

OTHER POEMS

BY

S. WEIR MITCHELL, M. D.

BOSTON
HOUGHTON, MIFFLIN AND COMPANY
New York: 11 East Seventeenth Street
The Riverside Press, Cambridge
1883

The Riverside Press, Cambridge:
Printed by H. O. Houghton and Company.

CONTENTS.

THE HILL OF STONES:

A LEGEND OF FONTAINEBLEAU.

WE two, my guide and I, through dusty ways
And formal avenues of well pruned trees,
Went past the village and thy dark gray walls,
Antique, deserted Fontainebleau; and still
With talk of him the shade of whose despair
Lies on thy court-yard yet, we loitering
Strolled through the deeper wood, and found
    at last
A barren space that crowned a hill's green
    slope,
Where, lonely as a king, a single oak,
Crippled in boisterous battle with the winds,
And gay with leafy flattery of the spring,
Seemed like an old man, cheated suddenly

1

With some sweet dream of childhood's tender
    hours.

" Here let us rest," he said, and casting down
His woodman's staff set out upon the grass
Twin flasks of Léoville and fair white loaves;
There as at ease we lay, and ate and drank,
My roving gaze in pleasant wanderings went
Down   the   green   hill, along the valley's
    range.

The noon-day sun hung half asleep in heaven,
And in the drowsied wood no leaflet's stir
Broke the still shadows slumbering on the
    ground.

Adown the hill, beside a brook that lay
A silver thread, heat-wasted, — far below,
Gaunt rocks in wild confusion tumbled lay,
Thick strewn along the narrowing vale, and barred
The distant thickets with their broken lines.
High on the further hill, twin mount to ours,
A single slab, time-worn, imperial, towered,

And all around it cumbering the sod
A stern gray host of barren rocks were cast
Each upon each, — as after battle lie
The dead upon the dead, to war no more, —
Whilst over them the hot and curdled air
Shook in uneasy whirls that broke the crests
Of distant trees and hill-tops far away.
In musing wonder tranced I lay and gazed
Down the cleft valley o'er the waste of stones, —
The while my comrade, stretched upon the
    grass,
Lay whistling cheerily his ballad gay
Of good king Dagobert; or smiling told,
With frequent urging, in his rough patois,
Some broken bit of legendary lore,
And at the last a story of these stones.

A thousand noisy years ago, 't is said,
Along yon silent vale at eventide
A bearded king, grown weary of the chase,

Rode thoughtful home, but pausing here awhile,
Said: " When life palls, and I no more can ride
With lance in rest, or smite with gleaming
     blade,
When sorrows sweeten the near cup of death,
Then in this valley's quiet I will build
A palace, where the wise and old shall come,
And none shall talk of what has been, and all
Shall ponder, with clear vision looking on
To that which is to be."
                Then pensive still
He turned away, and westward rode again,
Whilst after him an hundred barons came,
And riding swiftly, starred at intervals
The dark wood spaces with their robes of
     gold.
Next morn at Fontainebleau the bearded king
Held, neath the oaks, his court, when suddenly
A young knight, breaking through the outer
     guard,

Leapt featly from his jaded horse and cried,
Like one whom some dream-wonder spurs to
    speech :
" Good Sire, last night a lonely man I slept
Upon the hill you love ; and where at eve
The bald brown summit lay a dreary waste,
And where the sun of yesterday looked down
On utter solitude, and sowed the ground
With wild-eyed violets — O my liege, to-day
There stands a castle fair with courts and towers
And turrets tall and fretted pinnacles
Up-grown by night, in one still summer night,
As if fay-builded, and around it leap
A thousand soaring fountains, and the air
Reluctant from its bowered gardens floats
Sweet with strange odors. Underneath a porch
Of leaf carved masonry, I saw, my lord,
As peering through the thicket's fence I gazed,
The queen of women holding wondrous court
Of maidens only just less fair than she —

Herself the haughtiest woman of them all,
More cold and stately than her palace keep."
Then said the king : " The good knight's brain is
     crazed ;
Or hath he dreamed ? or do we live anew
An age of magic ? "

                    " Nay," the knight replied ;
" I dreamed it not ; " and smiled his bearded lord,
While merry laughter shook the mailed ring.
" Give me, good Sire, to seek again the hill,
And fill me with the beauty that doth glow
In her deep eyes, and either I will bring
This royal woman back again with me,
Or if there be delusion in my words,
The dream will break, and I ashamed shall come
To this fair court no more." Then as the king
In silence bent, he took his palfrey's rein,
And downward gazing parted wide the crowd,
And passed the yielding wood.

                  Whereon the king :

"The test is fair; 'tis chivalrous and just
That no man follow him;" and so with this
He went alone, and was no more with men.
Along the valley up the tufted sward
By cold-eyed statues underneath an arch
Of swaying fountains silently he went,
And half dismayed the rosy hedges broke,
And saw the lady and her maiden court.
Then there was sweet confusion, and a wood
Of white and shining arms in wonder raised,
And low quick modest cries from girls who fled
For shelter in the thickets, or took flight
Behind their queenly mistress. She alone
Towered, red and angry, one foot forward set.
"O woman wonderful," he cried — and bent
Before the tempest of her stormy eyes, —
"Send me not forth alone for aye, to hold
Thy memory only like a dagger sharp
To my sad heart; more sweet by far were
          death."

" Go, sir," she cried; " what right hast thou in
      me ?
Mine only is my beauty."   " Nay," he urged,
" Save that God put them in the world with us,
What right have we in yonder wide estate
Of sun and sky and flower haunted sod ? "
" No man on earth is peer of mine," she said, —
And saying this her cold eyes fell on him.
Her cold eyes fell on him; and deadly pale,
Bereft of thought, as one who gropes along,
He turned and went, whilst scornful laughter
      rang
From briery thickets everywhere around,
And chased his quick uncertain steps, that brake
The garden paths, till on the lone hill-side
A sudden coldness fettered limb and trunk,
And in his veins the liquid life grew still,
Whilst form and feature shrunk, and half way
      down
On the drear mountain side, a weight of stone

The knight at evening lay, to love no more.
Then quoth the waiting king as days went by:
"He hath not as he promised brought us back
The stately mistress of his fairy hall.
Who is there here, of all my lords, will seek
Yon magic palace, and with winsome wiles
And all the pleasant archery of love,
Fetch me this woman, captive of the heart?"
"And I, and I, and I," an hundred said;
And the sharp clangor of their shaken mail
Rang through the forest ways, as up they leapt.
So, one by one, as the cast die decreed,
They laughing went, and were no more with
    men.
But as the pleasant days of summer fled,
Thick clustered stones upon the hill-side marked
Where slept the flower of all that kingly court,
And heard no more the tread of dainty feet
Hail foot-falls round them, while the mellow
    tones

Of music floating from the terraced lawns
Struck echoes from their stony forms that lay
To wait their brothers when the curse should
     fall.
And so it chanced, that as the hill-side grew
Aghast with stony death, all living things
Its deadly boundaries fled, and man and beast
Turned from it ever with unquiet steps.
Yet now and then, when from a distant steep
The shepherd gazed, he saw some fated man
Climb with quick strides the hill, and through
     the stones
Depart from view; and looking then again,
Or hours or days thereafter, scared he saw
The same man, cold and palsied, issue forth
And reel and die, and smite the summer grass
With stony weight. And yet while men amazed
Stared, wondering that God and this could be,
The palace towers, ivy-curtained, stood
Unmoved and stern, as if a century long

Their breadth of shade, with each day's march,
    had crossed
The garden moats, and seen the lily buds
Unbosom tenderly to wild wind wooing
Each wanton morning of a hundred Junes;
Still ever through the silence of the night
A thousand fountains trembled high in air,
And not a breeze but rich as laden bee
Sailed from the garden, heavy with the freight
Of endless music, and the tender chime
Of cadenced voices, echoed high or low
From porch and hall and windowed gallery.

Again came June to lordly Fontainebleau,
And once again on field and woodland fell
The lazy lull of noontide drowsiness,
Where in cool caves of shadow slept the winds,
Whilst warm and still the moveless forest lay.
Therein betimes at fitful intervals,
The saintly quiet of this noonday trance,

Distant and grave, a solemn anthem filled,
And, soaring lark-like through the listening
    leaves
That trembled with its sorrow, died away;
But in its place a hymn rose, sweet and clear,
Such as at evening coming from the wells,
With balanced water-jars upon their heads,
The maidens sing.
             And thus from leafy shades
A knight full armed rode, singing as he went: —

    In olden days did Christ decree
    Twelve knightly hearts with him to be,
    And bade them wear no armor bright
    Save charity and conscience white.

    And through all lands they went and came,
    Not covetous of earthly fame,
    And gave the alms of Christian cheer
    To lowly serf and haughty peer.

For Christ they fought with word and prayer,
For Christ they died, — oh birthright fair !
Sweet Mary Mother grant to me
That I, like them, pure hearted be.

Then as the knight rode on through sun to shade,
And sang how good deeds, mightier than kings,
Are as the holy accolade of God,
And bid the poorest rise a knight of Christ,
From branch and thicket came the birds, and
     sailed ·
Around his silver casque, and caroling
Awoke the sleeping breezes, till he rode
With tossing plumes upon the open hill.
There all day long in silence wrapt, the knight
Knelt on the green turf gathering faith and
     strength ;
And all day long the same sweet retinue
Of summer songsters circled round his head.
When fell the night he rose and stern and calm,

Unlaced his armor slowly, piece by piece,
Laid down his helmet and his spurs of gold,
Ungirt his sword, and cast its jeweled weight
Beside his spear upon the burdened grass.
Then all unarmed and weaponless, he strode
Adown the hill, and sad and silent wound
Its cumbering stones among, till by the brook
Kneeling he crossed himself, and stayed no more,
But through the night, white robed and tranquil,
    went,
Passed in among the wood of founts that shook
Their silvery leafage in the moonlight gray,
Crossed with quick step the flower-beds, and
    passed
Where gleaming statues sentineled the path;
Then while the mirth rose wildest, and the
    sound
Of merry music shook the stems he touched,
He broke the rose-hedge, and untroubled stood
Amidst the wonder of the magic court.

Grave, glancing right and left, quoth he aloud:
" The peace of God, which passeth other peace,
Be on ye ever," — and so trembling stood
Dazed by the mystery of half seen limbs
And rosy secrets, chastened by the moon.
Swift moving through her shrinking court, the
    queen,
A head above them towering, flushed with wrath,
Shook from white neck and arms the roses red
That, ere he came, a hundred laughing girls
Showered from quick hands, which on a sudden
    checked,
Drooped with their flowery loads, — and " Sir,"
    she cried :
" Knightly it was, and noble thus to come;
Dost dream as others have to woo us home?"
" Most near the holy love of God," he said,
" Is such deep worship as a knightly heart
Doth give in some one woman unto all;
And whatsoever hath love's sweet disguise

Should in the tender eye of woman win
The gentle estimate of charity."
" A priest," she cried, — and smote the ground
    and shook
The lingering roses from her fallen hair ;
Upon the ground the good knight kneeling
    prayed :
" God grant," he murmured, " all my heart be
    pure,
Such love I give thee, woman, as thou hadst
For yonder stones, my brothers, they who lie
Awaiting God upon the mountain side."
" Enough," she cried ; " go, fool, and share with
    them
Their folly and their fate."   And so on him
Her cold-eyed anger fell, and still and chill
In the white moonlight they two stood and gazed
Each on the other, steady, eye to eye
And yet he went not, though through trunk and
    limb

The slow blood crept, and on his lip a prayer
Died in the saying.

         " Thou shalt go," she cried ;
And, bending, garnered from the flowery fence
A rosy handful. Then with scorn cast back
The snowy cloak that drifted from her neck,
And crying once a shrill and gnarled phrase,
Smote with the roses red his startled face.
On brow and cheek the flying roses struck,
And fell not down again, for suddenly
Twin petals flashed to wings ; and they who
     looked
Saw bud and blossom turned to flitting birds,
Which through the broken moonlight went and
     came,
And sang sweet carols round the white-robed
     knight,
This while the lady stood amazed and still ;
And all her court of wonder fettered maids
Like silence kept for fear, till at the last

2

The good knight, marveling, put out his hand,
And took the lady's finger tips, and went
With knightly courtesy and silent grace
Along the garden paths.   And as they passed,
Behind their steps the wind tossed grasses
      shrunk,
The flowers drooped, the noisy fountains ceased,
And vase and statue, fading into mist,
Went floating formless from the mountain top.
Still on they moved, she like a lily bent,
And all her women slowly followed her.
" Here pause," he said, and on the middle slope
Her trembling maids fell moaning round their
      Queen,
A silver ring upon the dark green turf.
" Behold morn waketh," said the knight; " no
      more,
No more for you shall any morning wake ;
I charge you look along yon valley drear."
Thereon she silent raised her head and gazed

Adown the hill-side thick with deathful stones,
And felt in heart and vein the pulsing blood
Stand still and curdle. So the hand he held
Stayed pointing down the valley, and he leapt
Across the ring of cold and moveless forms,
And walked in wonder down the mountain side,
And she and they stayed waiting on the hill
In endless horror gazing evermore, —
A tumbled heap of dreary rocks, that lay
About the statue of their stony Queen.

Very good, of the kind: but this kind of poetry is worse than useless.

Q. C. S,

"Truth, should be the basis of all literature"

Jno D. Thoreau,

WIND AND SEA.

Scene I.

*A June Afternoon. — Meadows. — A Farm, with distant
Woods; New Jersey Coast; Cape May.*

AN idle group within the willow's shade
We lay and chatted, holding lazy tilts,
And many a lance of mocking laughter broke,
Or calmly settled creeds and governments
High on the pleasant uplands of content,
Till soon the westering sun peeped underneath
The fringes of our green tent skirts, and fell,
Where on the paling-fence the milk cans gleamed
Red in the level gold, whilst suddenly,
Swift from the sea, the gay salt breezes came,
And, dipping like the swallows here and there,
With quick cool kisses touched the startled grain,

And fled ashamed, to seek new loves afar,
Where in the dark damp marsh the lilies float,
And lustrous leaved the white magnolia lifts
Its silvery censers, and the frogs, like friars,
Intone their even-song from stump and log.

HESTER (*rising*).

How sweet the air.   What was it that you sang
Of this same north wind's winter pranks?

The lusty north wind all night long
  His carols sang above my head,
And shook the roof, and roused the fire,
  And with the cold red morning fled.

Yet ere he left, upon my panes
  He drew, with bold and easy hand,
Pine and fir, and icy bergs,
  And frost ferns of his northern land;

And southward, like the Northmen old
  Whose ships he drove across the seas,

Has gone to fade where roses grow,
And die among the orange-trees.

ALFRED.

That 's music for a poet's soul, his words
Soft slipping from a woman's lips, the while
Caressed by lingering sunshine wrapt she stands,
A saintly aureole round her shining hair.

HENRY.

A bid for equal flattery. Let us go
Across the sand dunes o'er the mazy creeks.
Hear how old ocean calls us. Come away.

FRANK.

Dost thou remember that October day
We three together stood and saw at eve
The wanton wind yon sleeping Samson rouse,
Till at the touch of that coy courtesan
Strange yearnings seized him, and with shout
      and cry

He followed fleetly, while she, laughing, sought
The nodding golden-rods above the beach.

HENRY.

Ay, then it was you, perched beneath an oak,
To us, the long expectant heirs, set forth
King Autumn's testament and royal will.

HESTER.

I pray you tell again his dying thoughts,
And we shall lie upon the meadow grass
And be as heirs should be, stern visaged, grave,
Whilst you within yon bower of wild grapes
     stand :
So shall your words steal o'er the listening ear,
Breeze broken, while the melancholy sea
Moans his sad chorus on the distant shore.

FRANK.

Brown visaged Autumn sat within the wood,
And counted miserly his ripened wealth ;

The last crisped leaves sailed sauntering to earth,
The gentle winds stole by, and made no noise, —
Stole by on tip-toe, and the tree-frog shrill
Sang curfew to the nearly hidden moon.
I, Autumn, heritor of Summer's wealth, —
I, Autumn, who am old and near to death, —
Do thus make clear my will: I dowered earth
With fruit and flowers. I fed her hungry
    tribes,
The bee, the bird, the worm, the lazy flocks,
And like a king who unto certain death
Goes proudly clad, in royal state I go,
Through the long sunset of October woods,
Where like a trembling maid the smooth-limbed
    beech
Lets fall her ruddy robes, or where afield
Red vine leaves fleck the cedar's sombre cone,
Or where the maple and the hickory tall
Shed the long summer's store of garnered gold.
Mine, too, the orchard's raining fruit, and mine

Round-shouldered melons fattening in the sun;
Mine the brown pennons of the rustling maize,
The squirrel's nutty wealth, the crumpled gourd.
For I am Autumn, lord of fruits and flowers, —
God's almoner to all the tribes of man.
Here, then, to earth and all her habitants,
Dying, I leave what Summer's bounty gave:
Great store of grain, ripe fruit, and tasseled
    corn;
Yea, last of all, and best, I here bequeath,
With loving thought, a special legacy
To all good fellows everywhere on earth:
To them I give the sun-kissed grapes of Spain,
The Rhine's autumnal treasure, and the fruit
Of knightly Burgundy and winding Rhone;
Nor less the grape of Capri's lifted cliff,
The purple globes that jewel Ischia's isle,
And that sad vintage weeping holy tears
On black Vesuvius' breast. To them I give
The soothing sweetness of the Cuban leaf

Wherewith to hold good counsel, when life palls
Wherewith to charm away some weary hour.
And when from thoughtful lips the pale blue wreaths
Curl upward, or, the wanderer's only hearth,
His pipe-bowl, glows with hospitable fires,
I charge them drink a single cup, and say,
He was a good old fellow— peace to him.
So died great Autumn, passing like a mist,
Where in the woodland verge the maples rain
Reluctant gold in hesitating fall.

ALFRED (*to* HESTER).

See but our poet, all aglow he stands,
No light-house, 'mid the passion of the deep,
More still than he, amid his stir of thought.
What ho! good minstrel. Let us seaward roam,
'T is but a half hour's stroll past yonder hill.

FRANK.

I well recall the way. It lies within
A wood of stunted cedars and of firs,
Which heard in infancy the great sea moan,
And so took on the wilted forms of fright.

HESTER.

Well, too, I know it: when the tide is up
'T is barred and traversed by an hundred creeks,
So populous with lilies you might dream
King Oberon's navy rode at anchor there.

FRANK.

Let us away to it. Our sculptor here
Knows not the sea as we do. He shall feast
His eager eyes on. it, and own to us
That earth has glories other than the curves
Of lithe Apollo and the queen of love.

Scene II.

Sea Shore. — Sand Dunes dotted with stunted Trees.

HENRY.

Why never can the painter tell to us
This awful story of a lonely sea,
This terrible soliloquy of nature?
Why must he slip us in the bit of red,
The group of fishers or the tossing ship?
Who asks for life or human action here?

FRANK.

Nay, man is nature's complement. The sea,
The sky, the flowers suggest him. Well, I love
The smiling landscape of a woman's face,
So quaintly various, its two coy lakes,
Its rippling laughter, and its tearful showers.

ALFRED.

But he who worships nature, ought to be
The ready lover of her thousand gods,
His heart a home for every noble thought.

HESTER.

And such a thought is yon triumphant sea,
A thought, so statue like, so competent,
That I would leave it to its loneliness.

ALFRED.

Think what it was when unto God there came
This great sea thought.

FRANK.

       Here, friend, your chisel fails;
'T is powerless here. Thank Heaven, I at least
Can some way capture it with feeble brush.

ALFRED.

Alas 't is no man's prize. It mocks us all.
Leave me but only man, and you may paint,
And you may chisel. I would sail alone
The great Atlantic of the human heart.

HENRY.

Do you remember how, last summer, here
We played with fancies, and like idle lads
Struck to and fro the shuttlecocks of thought.

FRANK.

Ah, well I do. 'T was such an hour as comes
Once in the life of joy. Just here we lay,
As oft before you led the playful race.

HENRY.

Watch now the waves; each has his little life
High couraged triumph in his crest of pride,

Some proud decision in his onward sweep, —
Destruction, failure, — 't is a history !

FRANK.

And wilder yet, when of a winter day
The cold dry norther rolls athwart the beach
The gleaming foam balls into serpents white,
And all the sand is starred with rainbow lights.

HESTER.

It knoweth all the secrets of my moods:
To-day is gay with me, to-morrow grave.

FRANK.

And still for me sad always, — terrible,
As some God's grief beyond all earthly speech.

HESTER.

Lo wave on wave turns lapsing on the beach,
Like the great leaves of some eternal book.

ALFRED.

Unread forever. Lo, the sun has fled.

I pray you notice how the sea-side trees

Seem flying headlong, all their withering limbs

Stretched landward, craving refuge from the sea.

FRANK.

As they might be remorseful murderers,

That heard the hoarse deep, like to angry foes,

Storm up the sand slopes — nearer, nearer still,

Crying, vengeance, vengeance all the summer

    night.

THE SHRIVING OF GUINEVERE.

STILL she stood in the shunning crowd.
"Is there none," she said, aloud,
"None who knelt to me, great and proud,
Will say one word for me, sad and bowed?
Alas! it seems to me, if I
Were one of you, who, standing by,
Hear gathered in a woman's cry
The years of such an agony,
It seemeth me that I would take
Sweet pity's side for mine own sake,
And, knowing guilt alone should quake,
For chance of right one battle make."
But, no man heeding her, she stayed
Beneath the linden's trembling shade,
And peered, half hopeful, half afraid,
While passed in silence man and maid.

3

She, staring on the stone-dry street
Through the long summer-noonday heat,
And, stirring never from her seat,
Half saw men's shadows pass her feet.
" Ah me ! " she murmured, " well I see
How bitter each day's life may be
To them who have not where to flee
And are as one with misery."
But, whether knight to tourney rode,
Or bridal garments past her flowed,
Or by some bier slow mourners trode,
No sign of life the woman showed.

When as the priestly evening threw
The blessed waters of the dew,
About her head her cloak she drew
And hid her face from every view;
Till, as the twilight grew to shade,
And passed no more or man or maid,
A sudden hand was on her laid.

" And who art thou ? " she moaned, afraid ;
Beside her one of visage sad
Which yet to see made sorrow glad
Stood, in a knight's white raiment clad,
But neither sword nor poniard had.
" One who has loved you well," he said.
" Living I loved you well, and dead
I love you still; when joys were spread
Like flowers, and greatness crowned your head,
None loved you more. Not Arthur gave —
He will not check me from his grave —
So pure a love; nor Launcelot brave
With deeper love had yearned to save."
" Then," said the woman, still at bay,
" Why do I tremble when you lay
A hand upon my shoulder? Stay,
What is thy name, sir knight, I pray ?
For wheresoever memory chase
I know not one such troubled face,
Nor one that hath such godly grace

Of solemn sweetness any place :
But, whatsoever man thou be,
What is it I should do for thee ? "
Whereon, he, smiling cheerily,
Said : " I would have thee follow me."

Not any answer did he wait,
But turned towards the city gate ;
Not any word said she, but straight
Went after, bent and desolate ;
And, as a dream might draw, he drew
Her feet to action, till she knew
That house and palace round her grew,
And some wild revel's reeling crew,
And dame and page and squire and knight,
And torches flashing on the sight,
And fiery jewels flaming bright,
And love and music and delight ;
But slow across the spangled green
The stern knight went and went the queen, —

He solemn, silent, and serene,
She bending low with humble mien.
But where he turned the music died,
Love-parted lips no more replied,
And, shrinking back on either side,
Serf and lord stared, wonder-eyed,
Or marveling shrunk swift away
Before that visage solemn, gray,
Till, where the leaping fountains sway,
Thick showed the knights in white array.
There where he passed, though moved no breeze,
The leaves stirred trembling on the trees ;
And where he looked, by slow degrees
Fell silence and some strange unease,
Whilst whispers ran : " Who may it be ?
What knight is this ? And who is she ? "
But only Gawain looked to see,
And, praying, fell upon his knee.
Then said a voice full solemnly :
" Of all the knights that look on me,

If only one of them there be
That never hath sinned wittingly,
Let him the woman first disown,
Let him be first to cast a stone
At one, who, fallen from a throne,
Is sad and weary and alone.
Him, when the lists of God are set,
Him, when the knights of God are met,
If that he lacketh answer yet,
The soul of him shall answer get."

Then, as a lily bowed with rain
Leaps shedding it, she shed her pain,
And towering looked where men, like grain
Storm-humbled, bent upon the plain ;
Whilst over her the cold night air
Throbbed with some awful pulse of prayer,
As, bending low with reverent care,
She kissed the good knight's raiment fair.
When as she trembling rose again,

And felt no more in heart and brain
The weary weight of sin and pain,
For him that healed she looked in vain;
And from the starry heavens immense
Unto her soul with penitence
Came, as if felt by some new sense,
The noise of wings departing thence.

A TALE UNTOLD.

SWIFTLY over purple clover,
Through and under swaying leaves,
Past the brookside's dipping willows,
In among the upland sheaves,

Where the tumbled grasses sparkle,
Comes the wholesome northern breeze,
Shaking, breaking, mending shadows,
'Neath the thin leaved orchard trees.

Shut your eyes, dear love, I whispered,
While your own heart sings a song,
Something the wind shall tell, but haste —
Hide me not those sweet eyes long.

A song will come as your birds at call;
Fill it full of the mystic power
That climbs the sun-warmed trunks, and brings
Yearning dreams to bird and flower.

And so she lay with brown eyes shut,
Eyes more sweet than any be,
And murmured faint: The ships of thought
Come swift across a fairy sea.

Royal gifts thy galleons bring thee,
Ventures strange of sunset gold, —
Poet songs in love dreams murmured,
Cargoes rare of stories old.

Then passed her merry mood away; —
Love, she cried, not mine the tale,
By thought's swift stream I sit to hear
Its waters, that laugh or wail.

And love, I quake to hear how wild,
And sorrow to hear how sweet,
The murmured songs I cannot keep,
The thoughts that die at my feet.

Yet one quaint song I hold in thrall,
To tell ere the lordly freight
Shall perish with the fairy ships
Your fancy launched but of late.

An easy flow of warbled words,
Quaint as the antique tongue of birds,
Akin to theirs in likeness sweet,
Full thronged with meanings incomplete;
For she had shared, I think, with these,
Of nature's woodland mysteries;
Because, to hear her speech aright,
The booming bee would check his flight,
And, like to one in foreign lands,
Who hears a tongue he understands,

The startled swallow dipped so near
He almost touched my lady's ear.
Love-treason were it I should tell
The charm-words of that dainty spell;
As lief would I, if well I knew
 The secret of each forest bower,
Their virgin whispers tell to you,
 To while away a common hour.
Or could I learn what gracious words
Wake up betimes the drowsy birds,
When in the first-born morning breeze
Take exercise the stately trees,
With great limbs swinging full of strength,
As when a giant's easy length
Doth take delight on buoyant seas.
'T were vain to ask with me to share
The thoughts of earth, or sea, or air,
Because their voice to understand
You must have been sea, air, or land.
But if the riddle sound untrue,

Some woman witch will read it you.
So is it I would only share
With woodland folk her song of prayer, —
With these plumed citizens of June,
Her echoes of their joyous tune ;
With them alone the graver chants
That roused their choir in orchard haunts,
And answered with a loving grace
The challenge of my yearning face.

KEARSARGE [1]

SUNDAY in Old England:
  In gray churches everywhere
The calm of low responses,
  The sacred hush of prayer.

Sunday in Old England;
  And summer winds that went
O'er the pleasant fields of Sussex,
  The garden lands of Kent,

Stole into dim church windows
  And passed the oaken door,

[1] On Sunday morning, June 19, 1864, the noise of the cannons during the fight between the Kearsarge and the Alabama was heard in English churches near the Channel.

And fluttered open prayer-books
  With the cannon's awful roar.

Sunday in New England:
  Upon a mountain gray
The wind-bent pines are swaying
  Like giants at their play;

Across the barren lowlands,
  Where men find scanty food,
The north wind brings its vigor
  To homesteads plain and rude.

Ho, land of pine and granite!
  Ho, hardy northland breeze!
Well have you trained the manhood
  That shook the Channel seas,

When o'er those storied waters
  The iron war-bolts flew,

And through Old England's churches
  The summer breezes blew;

While in our other England
  Stirred one gaunt rocky steep,
When rode her sons as victors,
  Lords of the lonely deep.

HOW THE CUMBERLAND WENT DOWN.

GRAY swept the angry waves
  O'er the gallant and the true,
Rolled high in mounded graves
  O'er the stately frigate's crew —
Over cannon, over deck,
Over all that ghastly wreck, —
    When the Cumberland went down.

Such a roar the waters rent
  As though a giant died,
When the wailing billows went
  Above those heroes tried;
And the sheeted foam leaped high,
Like white ghosts against the sky, —
    As the Cumberland went down.

O shrieking waves that gushed
    Above that loyal band,
Your cold, cold burial rushed
    O'er many a heart on land!
And from all the startled North
A cry of pain broke forth,
      As the Cumberland went down.

And forests old, that gave
    A thousand years of power
To her lordship of the wave
    And her beauty's regal dower,
Bent, as though before a blast,
When plunged her pennoned mast,
      And the Cumberland went down.

And grimy mines that sent
    To her their virgin strength,
And iron vigor lent,
    To knit her lordly length,

4

Wildly stirred with throbs of life,
Echoes of that fatal strife,
 As the Cumberland went down.

Beneath the ocean vast,
 Full many a captain bold,
By many a rotting mast,
 And admiral of old,
Rolled restless in his grave
As he felt the sobbing wave,
 When the Cumberland went down.

And stern Vikings that lay
 A thousand years at rest,
In many a deep blue bay
 Beneath the Baltic's breast,
Leaped on the silver sands,
And shook their rusty brands,
 As the Cumberland went down.

HERNDON.

Ay, shout and rave, thou cruel sea,
  In triumph o'er that fated deck,
Grown holy by another grave —
  Thou hast the captain of the wreck.

No prayer was said, no lesson read,
  O'er him, the soldier of the sea;
And yet for him, through all the land,
  A thousand thoughts to-night shall be.

And many an eye shall dim with tears,
  And many a cheek be flushed with pride;
And men shall say, There died a man,
  And boys shall learn how well he died.

Ay, weep for him, whose noble soul
  Is with the God who made it great;
But weep not for so' proud a death, —
  We could not spare so grand a fate.

Nor could Humanity resign
  That hour which bade her heart beat high,
And blazoned Duty's stainless shield,
  And set a star in Honor's sky.

O dreary night! O grave of hope!
  O sea, and dark, unpitying sky!
Full many a wreck these waves shall claim
  Ere such another heart shall die.

Alas, how can we help but mourn
  When hero bosoms yield their breath!
A century itself may bear
  But once the flower of such a death;

So full of manliness, so sweet
  With utmost duty nobly done;
So thronged with deeds, so filled with life,
  As though with death that life begun.

It *has* begun, true gentleman!
  No better life we ask for thee;
Thy Viking soul and woman heart
  Forever shall a beacon be, —

A starry thought to veering souls,
  To teach it is not best to live;
To show that life has naught to match
  Such knighthood as the grave can give.

THE QUAKER GRAVEYARD.

Four straight brick walls, severely plain,
  A quiet city square surround;
A level space of nameless graves, —
  The Quakers' burial-ground.

In gown of gray, or coat of drab,
  They trod the common ways of life,
With passions held in sternest leash,
  And hearts that knew not strife.

To yon grim meeting-house they fared,
  With thoughts as sober as their speech,
To voiceless prayer, to songless praise,
  To hear their elders preach.

Through quiet lengths of days they came,
  With scarce a change to this repose;
Of all life's loveliness they took
  The thorn without the rose.

But in the porch and o'er the graves,
  Glad rings the southward robin's glee,
And sparrows fill the autumn air
  With merry mutiny;

While on the graves of drab and gray
  The red and gold of autumn lie,
And willful Nature decks the sod
  In gentlest mockery.

LINES TO A DESERTED STUDY.

Hush! Feel ye not around us teem
The shapes that haunted Goethe's dream?
When lifted genius mused apart,
And taste inspired the soul of art;
Young first Love, coy with trembling wings,
And Hope, the lark that soaring sings,
And boyhood friendships prone to fade
Through pleasant zones of sun and shade;
With many a phantom born of youth,
The trust in honor, faith, and truth
That fails in after years;
The perfect pearls of life's young dream
Dissolved in manhood's tears.
Through Time's swift loom our joys and griefs
In braided strands together run;

To weave about this world of ours
Wild tapestries of shade and sun.
And seems it not as if to-night,
Dear, dusty, many-memoried room,
Our souls had lost the threads of light,
And like the eve kept gathering gloom?
Ay, and for one of us the hour
Must have, methinks, a double power,
As backward turns his saddened look,
To view again those many scenes,
When life was like an uncut book,
And Joy was in her rosy teens.
Yes, even we who later knew
The home of friendship and of taste,
Stand saddened by the parting view
Of scenes by recollection graced.
Ah, there the books looked meekly out
Above an alligator's snout;
And bugs and fossils, birds and bones,
Round-shouldered bottles, jars, and stones,

Stood up in order sage, —
Memorials they of every clime,
Remains of every age.
Oh, yes, 't was here at eventide
We lingered by the table's side,
Whilst Wit her lightning stories told,
And through Havana's clouds of gold
The thunder-storm of laughter rolled,
Till Mirth her very contrast brought,
And drooped the brow in earnest thought;
While tranced we sat, as now we sit,
And fast the parting time draws near,
And these stained walls seem gathering grace
As if to grow more doubly dear;
And not an ink-mark on the boards
But wears a half-appealing look.
The mottled wall, the naked floor,
I read them as ye read a book, —
As if they something had to say,
And sought but could not find a way;

As often 'mid the waning year,
In brown-cheeked autumn's bowers,
The leaves ye tread seem rustling low, —
Tread gently, we were flowers.

ELK COUNTY.

FROM lands of the elk and the pine-tree,
Of hemlock and whitewood and maple,
You ask me to write you a lyric
Shall thrill with the cries of the forest,
And flow like the sap of the maple, —
The rich yellow blood of the maple,
That hath such a wild, lusty sweetness,
Such a taste of the wilderness in it.
And surely 't were pleasant to summon
The days which so lately have vanished,
The friends who were part of their pleasure.
Right cheery for me, in the city,
To think once again of the sunsets
We watched from the crest of the hill-top,
Alone on the stumps in the clearing;

When all the grand slopes of the mountains,
Our own hills, our loved Alleghanies,
Grow hazy and drowsy and solemn,
Cloaked each with the shade of his neighbor;
Like rigid old Puritans scorning
The passion and riot of color,
Of yellow and purple and scarlet,
Which haunt the gay court of the sunset,
Where Eve, like a wild Cinderella,
Awaits the gray fairy of twilight.
Sweet, ever, to think of the forests,
Their cool, woody fragrance delicious;
To think of the camp fires we builded
To baffle those terrible pungies;
To think how we wandered, bewildered
With wood-dreams and delicate fancies
Unknown to the life of the city.
To tread but those cushioning mosses;
To lie, almost float, on the fern-beds;
To feel the crisp crush of the foot on

The mouldering logs of the windfall,

Were things to be held in remembrance.

Dost recall how we lingered to listen

The sound of the wood-robin's bugle,

Or bent the witch-hopple to guide us,

As one folds the page he is reading,

And felt, as we peered through the stillness,

Through armies and legions of tree-trunks,

Such solemn and brooding sensations

As told of the birth of religions,

As whispered how men grow to Druids

When the fly-wheel of work is arrested,

And they live but the life of the forest?

Ay, here in the face of the woodman,

You see how the woods have been preaching,

As he leans on the logs of his cabin

To watch the prim city-folk coming

O'er the chips, and the twigs, and the stubble,

Through the fire-scarred stumps, and the hem-
    locks

His axe hath so ruthlessly girdled.
Ay, he too has learned in the forest,
One half of him Nimrod and slayer,
Unsparing, enduring, and tireless,
In wait for the deer at the salt lick;
Yet one stronger half of his nature —
This rough and bold out-of-door nature,
Hath touches of sadness upon it,
And is grown to the ways of the forest,
Till wildness and softness together
Are one with the sap of his being.

Right pleasant it were, friend and lady,
To tell you some tale of the woodland;
To hear the faint voice of tradition,
Of childish and simple conceptions,
And find in their half-spoken meanings
Some thought all the nations have muttered
In the parable tongues of their childhood.
But alas for the tale and the writer!

The land has no story to tell us, —
No voice save the Clarion's waters,
No song save the murm'rous confusion
Of winds gone astray in the pine-tops,
Or the roar of the rain on the hemlocks; —
No record, no sign, not a word of
The lords of the axe and the rifle,
Who camped by the smooth Alleghany,
And blazed the first tree on the mountain.
Yet here, even here in the forest, —
The soul-calming deep of the forest,
Where cat-birds are noisy and dauntless,
And deft little miserly squirrels
Are hoarding the beech-nuts for winter;
Where rattlesnakes charm, and the hoot-owl
By night sounds his murderous war-pipe, —
Yes, here in the last home of Nature,
Where the greenness that swells o'er the hillock
Is pink with the blossoming laurel,
The wants of the city still haunt us,

When busy blue axes are ringing,
And totter the kings of the mountain.
Ah, well you recall, I can fancy,
The morn we looked down on the valley
That bears the proud name of the battle,
Itself a fair field for the winning;
Recall, too, the frank speech which told us
Who felled the first tree in the valley
Where now the red heifers are browsing,
And reapers are swinging their cradles,
And fat grow the stacks with the harvest.
Canst see, too, the dam and the mill-pond,
The trees in the dark amber water,
Where thousands of pine logs are tethered,
With maple and black birch and cherry?
Canst hear, as I hear, the gay hum of
The bright whizzing saw in the steam-mill,
Its up-and-down old-fashioned neighbor
Singing, " Go it ! " and " Go it ! " and " Go it ! "
As it whirrs through the heart of the pine-tree.

And spouts out the saw-dust, and filleth
The air with its resinous odors ?
Ay, gnaw at them morning and evening,
Thou hungry old dog of a saw-mill!
The planks thou art shaping so deftly
Shall ring with the tramp of the raftsmen,
Shall drift on the shallow Ohio,
Shall build thy fair homes, Cincinnati,
Shall see the gay steamers go by them,
Shall float on the broad Mississippi,
Shall floor the rough cabins of Kansas.

And here is a tale for the poet, —
A story of Saxon endurance,
A story of work and completion,
A legend of rough-handed labor
As wild as the runes of the fiords.

CAMP-FIRE LYRICS.

A CAMP IN THREE LIGHTS.

AGAINST the darkness sharply lined
  Our still white tents gleamed overhead,
And dancing cones of shadow cast
  When sudden flashed the camp-fire red,

Where fragrant hummed the moist swamp-spruce,
  And tongues unknown the cedar spoke,
While half a century's silent growth
  Went up in cheery flame and smoke.

Pile on the logs! A flickering spire
  Of ruby flame the birch-bark gives,
And as we track its leaping sparks,
  Behold in heaven the North-light lives!

An arch of deep, supremest blue,
　　A band above of silver shade,
Where, like the frost-work's crystal spears,
　　A thousand lances grow and fade,

Or shiver, touched with palest tints
　　Of pink and blue, and changing die,
Or toss in one triumphant blaze
　　Their golden banners up the sky,

With faint, swift, silken murmurings,
　　A noise as of an angel's flight,
Heard like the whispers of a dream
　　Across the cool, clear northern night.

Our pipes are out, the camp-fire fades,
　　The wild auroral ghost-lights die,
And stealing up the distant wood
　　The moon's white spectre floats on high,

And, lingering, sets in awful light
    A blackened pine-tree's ghastly cross,
Then swiftly pays in silver white
    The faded fire, the aurora's loss.

NIGHT — LAKE HELEN.

I LIE in my red canoe
    On the waters still and deep,
And o'er me darkens the sky,
    And beneath the billows sleep;

Till, between the stars above
    And those in the lake's embrace,
I seem to float like the dead
    In the noiselessness of space.

Betwixt two worlds I drift,
    A bodiless soul again, —

Between the still thoughts of God
  And those which belong to men;

And out of the height above,
  And out of the deep below,
A thought that is like a ghost
  Doth gather and gain and grow,

That now and forevermore
  This silence of death shall hold,
While the nations fade and die,
  And the countless years are. rolled.

But I turn the light canoe,
  And, darting across the night,
Am glad of the paddles' noise
  And the camp-fire's honest light.

NIPIGON LAKE.

HIGH-SHOULDERED and ruddy and sturdy,
Like droves of pre-Adamite monsters,
The vast mounded rocks of red basalt
Lie basking round Nipigon's waters;
And still lies the lake, as if fearing
To trouble their centuried slumber;
And heavy o'er lake and in heaven
A dim veil of smoke tells of forests
Ablaze in the far lonely Northland:
And over us, blood-red and sullen,
The sun shines on gray-shrouded islands,
And under us, blood-red and sullen,
The sun in the dark umber water
Looks up at the gray, murky heaven,
While one lonely loon on the water
Is wailing his mate, and beside us
Two shaggy-haired Chippewa children
In silence watch sadly the white man.

EVENING STORM — NIPIGON.

UPON the beach, with low, quick, mournful sob,
The weary waters shudder to our feet;
And far beyond the sunset's golden light,
Forever brighter in its lessening span,
Shares not the sadness of yon grim wood-wall,
Whose dark and noiseless deeps of shadow rest
In sullen gloom 'twixt golden lake and sky.
Shine out, fair light, in yellow glory shine!
Fast fades the lessening day, and far beneath
The tamarack shivers and the cedar's cone
Uneasy sways, while fitful tremors stir
The tattered livery of the ragged birch;
And over all the arch of heaven is wild
With tumbled clouds, where fast the lightning's
   lance
Gleams ruby red and thunder-echoes roll;
Whilst yet below — sweet as the dream of hope

What time despair is nearest — lies the lake.
Fast comes the storm; spiked black with patter-
    ing rain,
The darkened water gleams with bells of foam.
Fast comes the storm, till over lake and sky,
O'er yellow lake and ever-yellowing sky,
Cruel and cold, the gray storm-twilights rest;
And so the day before its time is dead.

NOONDAY WOODS — NIPIGON.

BETWEEN thin fingers of the pine
    The fluid gold of sunlight slips,
And through the tamarack's gray-green fringe
    Upon the level birch leaves drips.

Through all the still, moist forest air
    Slow trickles down the soft, warm sheen,
And flecks the branching wood of ferns
    With tender tints of pallid green,

To rest where close to mouldered trunks
  The red and purple berries lie,
Where tiny jungles of the moss
  Their tropic forests.rear on high.

Fast, fast asleep the woodland rests,
  Stirs not the tamarack's topmost sheaf,
And slow the subtle sunlight glides
  With noiseless step from leaf to leaf.

And lo, he comes! the fairy prince,
  The heir of richer, softer strands:
A summer guest of sterner climes,
  He moves across the vassal lands.

And lo, he comes! the fairy prince,
  The joyous sweet southwestern breeze:
He bounds across the dreaming lake,
  And bends to kiss the startled trees,

Till all the woodland wakes to life,
    The pheasant chirps, the chipmunks cry,
And scattered flakes of golden light
    Athwart the dark wood-spaces fly.

Ah, but a moment, and away!
    The fair, false prince has kissed and fled:
No more the wood shall feel his touch,
    No more shall know his joyous tread.

PADDLE-SONG.[1]

THE mist is thick, the waters quick,
    And fast we flit along;
The foam-bells flash, the paddles splash, —
    Sing us a merry song.

What's this I see come swift to me
    Across the rapids dark?

[1] Freely rendered from a Canadian *chanson.*

A princess fair, with yellow hair,
  A red canoe of bark.

Her golden hair floats thick and fair
  Far, far behind her lee,
And pike and trout come leaping out,
  Her merry locks to see.

With a silver gun, a silver gun,
  The tall white swan she slew:
He moaned a hymn, his sight grew dim,
  It might have been I or you.

The feathers, white as the still moonlight,
  Toss red on the waters free,
And gay trout break the silent lake,
  The small white boats to see.

The silver ball has found his heart:
  It might have hit you or me.

The round white ball has found his heart:
  Ah sad! ah sad to see!

Quick is the flash of her paddle's dash,
  And far and free behind,
In the roar and splash of the rapids' crash,
  Her hair floats on the wind.

Turn not to view her swift canoe;
  Ave Maria! beware! beware!
Look not behind, where wave and wind
  Roll out her rippled hair.

AFTER SUNSET — LAKE WEELOKENEBAKOK.

At twilight Azescohos lieth
With domes that are builded of color:
Its deep-wrinkled strata and bowlders,
Its sombre-leaved greenness of noonday,
Fade lost in the blue misty splendor

That seems like the soul of a color ;
While far, far away to the eastward
One vast fading glory of scarlet —
A color that seems as if living —
Possesses the sky like a passion,
And higher and higher in heaven
Fades out in the soft bluish greenness
That climbs to the zenith above us.
Below, far below, as if thinking,
At rest lies the sensitive lake ; and
Like one who sings but to her own heart
Such thoughts as a loving lip whispers,
So deep in the waters are pictured
The beauty of sunset and hill-side.
For the blue that was blue on the mountain,
Seen deep in the heart of the water,
Hath the touch of some blessing upon it, —
Some strangeness of purity in it,
Like color that shall be in heaven.
This water-held vision of sunset,

Ablaze in the depths of the darkness,
Is it but for the sight? Canst not hear it,
This prophet of color, to tell us
Of what may be yet, when the senses
Awaken to lordlier being,
And the thought of the blind man is ours?
When colors unearthly men know not
Shall float from. the trumpets of angels,
And tints of the glory of heaven
Shall be for us color and music?

FRAGMENT OF A CHIPPEWA LEGEND.

DESPAIRING and sunburnt and thirsty,
The forest-trees bend o'er the lake-brink,
Where, mocking them, chatter the squirrels
At play on the mouldering mosses;
While over them, blue and relentless,
Rise, cloudless and sultry, the heavens.
And where, cried the pine-tree in anger,
Ah, where is my warrior North Wind?
Asleep, quoth the gossiping chipmunk,
On white-bosomed snows of the Northland.
And where, moaned the glossy-limbed beeches,
Where hide our sweet chiefs of the summer,
The rose-breathing South and the West Wind?
Shrilled sharply the loon, from the water,
In gardens of jasmine they wander,

In tents of the lily they linger.
Spake sadly the tamarack stately :
O'er forest and mountain top vainly
A-weary I watch for the East Wind, —
My wild warring rover, the East Wind,
Who smites the dark sea in his fury,
And comes to me eager and angry.
Forgotten, forgotten, forgotten,
The nightingale [1] sings from the elders.

[1] The Canadian nightingale; so called by the *voyageurs.* I have never heard him sing at night.

6

THE MARSH.

SAFELY moored on the dappled water,
　　The broad green lily-pads dip and sway,
While, like a skipper, a gray frog rides
　　The biggest leaf in the tiny bay.

Merrily leap the brown-cheeked waves
　　To seize the sunlight's liberal gold,
Which shakes and flickers among the reeds,
　　And on the stones of the beach is rolled.

O'er marish meadows, and far beyond,
　　Silken and green or velvety gray,
Tufted grasses with shifting colors
　　In the wholesome north wind toss and play.

Lonely and sad, on the sea of green,
   The cardinal-flower a light-house stands, —
A scarlet blaze in the morning sun,
   To guide the honey-bees' toiling bands.

What was it for, this flower's beauty,
   Its royal color's marvelous glow?
Not, like a good deed, still rejoicing
   The soul that grew it, though no one know.

All unconscious, only a flower,
   Life without zest, and death without thought;
Lost as a stone to the sweet, deep pleasure
   Its scarlet wonder to me has brought.

Has it, I ponder, no sense of pleasing,
   No least estate in the world of joy?
Have the leaf and the grass no conscious sense
   Of what they give us, — no want or cloy?

Not so unlike us. The words that weight us
  With keenest sorrow and longest pain
Fall oft from lips that rest unconscious
  If that they give us be loss or gain.

Do I only have power to fill me
  From sun and flower with joy intense?
Has yon cold frog on his lonely leaf raft
  No lower share through a duller sense?

Think you the ladies he woos are sought
  For form, or color, or beauty's sake?
That, touched with sorrow, he mourns to-day
  Some mottled Helen beneath the lake?

Why should fret us this constant riddle,
  To know if Nature be kind or harsh
To the pensive frog on his green-ribbed float,
  The scarlet queen of the lonely marsh?

Haply, in thought-spheres far above us,
 Some may watch us with larger powers,
Asking if we have wit or reason,
 Asking if pain or joy be ours.

But *does* it vex me, this endless riddle
 I toss about in my helpless brain,
To know if life be worth the having,
 If just mere being be any gain?

Scarce can I answer. Something surely
 The thought has brought me this summer
 morn, —
Something for me in life were missing
 If frog and flower had ne'er been born.

A CONCEIT.

LOITERING scents from the garden come,
  Blown from shelter of wind-stirred trees;
Like bits of song from the lips we love,
  They rise and fade on the evening breeze.

And shall we marry in wedlock sweet
  The poet's soul and the floweret's breath,
And, musing, wonder what many tongues
  The yearning singer may gain in death?

Who wilt thou hear in the rich wild scents
  Of the ancient gardens' well-trimmed shade?
Who shall the jessamine's laureate be,
  And who for the summer's noble maid?

The great red rose shall tell us in song
  Her tender passion of sweet perfume;
And whose shall the frail clematis be,
  With its faint aroma and fringe of bloom?

Wilt give unto Keats the waiting rose;
  To Shelley's voice the violet's scent;
And Spenser's measure of stately song,
  To haunt the lily's silvery tent.

MILAN.

DA VINCI'S CHRIST.

ALL day long, year after year,
  Maid and man and priest and lay
Wander in from crowded streets,
  And through the long, cool gallery stray.

And with them, in the fading light,
  We loiter past the pictured wall,
Till lo! a face before us comes,
  And something wistful seems to fall

From two strange eyes that stay all steps;
  For here a priest, and there a maid,
Two lads, a soldier, and a *bonne*,
  Before the rail their steps have stayed.

What message bore this awful face,
　Through all the waning centuries fled?
What says it to the gazer now?
　What said it to the myriad dead

Who came and went like us to-day,
　And, pausing here in silence, all
In silence laid their weight of sins
　Before this grand confessional?

A face more sad man never dreamed,
　A face more sweet man never wrought;
So solemn-sad, so solemn-sweet,
　Serenely set in quiet thought.

The silent sunlight slips away,
　The soldiers pass, the *bonne* goes by;
The painter drapes his copy in,
　And stops his work and heaves a sigh.

And followed by those eyes, that have
   The patience of eternity,
We carry to the bustling street
   Their loving *Benedicite.*

BRUGES: QUAI DES AUGUSTINS.

(AFTER VAN DER VEER.)

WITHIN the sad, deserted street,
   We stand a little space to gaze,
Beneath the high-walled garden's shade,
   Amid the twilight's growing haze.

The still depths of the dark canal,
   Between gray walls of ancient stone,
Stir not to any wind that blows,
   And seem so silent, so alone,

We wonder at the lazy swans
   That o'er the water dare to glide,
And marvel at the lads who cast
   Their pebbles from the bridge's side.

Quaint houses bound the darksome wave,
　Time-tinted, yellow, umber, gray,
With gaping gargoyles overhead,
　And underneath sweet gardens gay,

With ivy, flung like cloaks of green
　Upon the worn and mottled wall;
Forgotten centuries ago
　By burgher dames at even-fall.

Across the narrow space of flowers,
　A maid in scarlet petticoat
Comes with her shining pail of brass,
　And bends above the moveless moat;

And breaks her image with the pail,
　And scares the swans, and trips away,
And leaves the stern, gray, sombre street
　To silence and the waning day.

NEAR AMSTERDAM.

(AFTER ALBERT CUYP.)

SOBER gray skies and ponderous clouds,
　With gaps between of pallid blues;
Bluff breezes stirring the brown canal;
　A broad, flat meadow's myriad hues

Of soft and changeful breadths of green,
　Barred with the silvery grass that bows
By straight canals, and dotted o'er
　With black and white of basking cows;

And distant sails of hidden ships
　The ceaseless windmills show or hide,
And through the languid willows gleam,
　And over red-tiled houses glide.

Two sturdy lads with wooden shoes,
  Go clumping down the reed-fringed dyke,
And tow a broad-bowed boat, where dreams
  The quaint, sweet virgin of Van Eyck.

And slipt from out the revel high,
  Where gay Franz Hals has bid him sit,
Above the bridge, his lazy pipe
  Smokes placidly the stout De Witt.

NEAR UTRECHT.

(AFTER TENIERS.)

A QUIET curve of sombre brown water,
    Flecked with duck-weed and dotted with
      leaves;
A low brick cottage, where shadows nestle
    'Neath velvet edges of well-thatched eaves.

In front a space, with its gaudy dahlias
    And solid shade of the branching lime,
Where, soberly gay, two boors are drinking
    In the deep'ning gloom of the evening time.

ON A PICTURE BY ALBERT CUYP.

A SUNSET silence holds the patient land;
Against the sun the stolid cattle stand;
Framed hazy, in the gold that slips
Between the sails of lazy ships,
And floods with level yellow light
The broad green meadow grasses bright.

AMSTERDAM GALLERY.

(AFTER RUYSDAEL.)

THROUGH briery ways, from underneath
　　The far-off sadness of the gold
That fades above the sun, the waves
　　Swift to our very feet are rolled.

Above, beyond, to either side,
　　The sombre woods bend overhead;
And underneath, the wild brown waves
　　Leap joyously, with lightsome tread,

From rock to rock, and laugh and sing,
　　Like lonely maids in woods at play;
Till in the cold, still pool below,
　　A-sudden checked they stand at bay,

7

Like girls who, in their mood of joy,
 To this more solemn woodland glide,
And with some brief, sweet terror touched,
 Stand wistful, trembling, tender-eyed.

What half-felt sense of something gone,
 What sadness in the moveless woods ;
What sorrow haunts yon amber sky,
 That over all so darkly broods !